ELLIS ISLAND

ELLIS ISLAND

DILLON PRESS
New York

Maxwell Macmillan Canada
Toronto

Maxwell Macmillan International
New York Oxford Singapore Sydney

By Catherine Reef

30036000933596

Photographic Acknowledgments

Special thanks to Peter B. Kaplan, who supplied all the contemporary photographs that appear in this book. Mr. Kaplan is the preferred photographer for the Statue of Liberty-Ellis Island Foundation, Inc. His daughter, Ricki Liberty Kaplan, born in 1987, was named after the Statue of Liberty.

The aerial photographs in chapter one and on the title page have been reproduced through the courtesy of James Blank.

The historical photographs have been reproduced through the courtesy of the Library of Congress and the National Archives.

Cover photograph courtesy of the National Park Service.

Library of Congress Cataloging-in-Publication Data

Reef, Catherine.
   Ellis Island / by Catherine Reef.
      p. cm. — (Places in American history)
   Includes index.
   Summary: Reviews the history of the immigration center where more than twelve million immigrants became new Americans over a sixty-year period.
   ISBN 0-87518-473-1
   1. Ellis Island Immigration Station (New York, N.Y.)—History—Juvenile literature. [1. Ellis Island Immigraton Station (New York, N.Y.)—History. 2. United States—Emigration and immigration—History.] I. Title II. Series.
   JV6484.R44 1991
   325' .1'0973—dc20   91-18755

Dillon Press
Macmillan Publishing Company
866 Third Avenue
New York, NY 10022

Maxwell Macmillan Canada, Inc.
1200 Eglinton Avenue East
Suite 200
Don Mills, Ontario M3C 3N1

Macmillan Publishing Company is part of the Maxwell Communication Group of Companies.

First edition
Printed in the United States of America
10   9   8   7   6   5   4   3   2   1

CONTENTS

PLACES IN AMERICAN HISTORY

Ellis Island

Hudson River

Manhattan

East River

Jersey City

Ellis Island

Battery Park

New York City

Statue of Liberty

Liberty Island

Governors Island

Brooklyn

Upper New York Bay

New Jersey

New York

Staten Island

to Atlantic Ocean

N

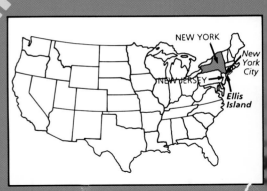

NEW YORK

New York City

NEW JERSEY

Ellis Island

CHAPTER 1

ENTERING AMERICA'S GATE

The steamship sailed from a German port on May 13, 1920. Its three hundred passengers had paid twenty-five dollars each for their passage across the Atlantic Ocean to America. These people were immigrants. They had fled hunger and suffering in search of a better life. They came from different countries, including Russia, Romania, and Poland, and they spoke different languages. Yet they all had something in common—each hoped to make America his or her new home.

During the voyage, storms kept the immigrants from coming up on deck. Most people became seasick, and many wondered about the wisdom of leaving their native country.

On the seventh morning at sea, the sun broke through the clouds and the people came up from below. They crowded up on deck, breathing fresh air for the first time in days. And then the cry arose: There it is!

In the distance was a little dot on the horizon. As the ship moved closer, it got bigger and bigger—it was the Statue of Liberty. Her torch gleamed golden in the morning sunlight. "Lady Liberty!" the people shouted. They started laughing and singing. Some wept tears of joy. The welcoming Statue of Liberty seemed to promise that all of the immigrants' dreams would come true. But their trip was not yet over.

Just to the north of the Statue of Liberty was another well-known place—Ellis Island. As the passengers gazed out at this tiny island, they grew strangely quiet. Ellis Island was called the Gateway to America, but it was also called the Island of Tears. On this island, the United States government would decide whether the

An aerial view of modern day Ellis Island, the small square island (on the left) just north of the Statue of Liberty.

passengers would be allowed to stay in America or be sent back to their homelands.

The immigrants' ship docked in New York Harbor, and they were herded onto a ferry bound for Ellis Island. Dozens of ferries carrying hundreds of people made this trip to Ellis Island each day.

In all, about fifteen million immigrants were processed through Ellis Island between 1892 and 1954. Many had never been outside their villages before. Most didn't speak English, had very little money, and had left their families behind. Golda Meir, who later became the prime minister of Israel, emigrated from Russia in 1906 when she was eight. Golda said that coming to this unknown land was "almost like going to the moon!"

Most immigrants never returned to the land of their birth. One man remembers that his mother was crying very hard just before he left. He couldn't understand why. Years later he said,

"I understand it now. I never saw her again."

Many times, a whole village pitched in to raise the money for a family's eldest son or daughter to buy a ticket to America. The immigrant would find work and after many months send back the sum borrowed. Then he or she would work to raise money to buy a ticket to bring other family members to America. Over a period of years, families emigrated in this way.

More immigrants were processed on Ellis Island than anywhere else in America. Almost half of the citizens living in the United States today—one hundred million—are descended from immigrants who passed through Ellis Island's Registry Building.

Inside the huge three-story redbrick and concrete main building, immigration officers calling out in different languages directed the immigrants through their inspections. If the officials decided that the people were healthy and able to work, they were allowed to enter the country.

Most immigrants passed the inspection. They settled in cities and towns across America. They took whatever jobs were available, often working seven days a week for twelve hours a day. They helped build America's railroads, worked in factories and on farms, and started their own businesses.

Beginning in 1921, the government set limits on the number of immigrants who could come to America. At one time, over eleven thousand people had passed through Ellis Island in a day. Once the new laws took effect, that many didn't come through in one week.

By 1954 people who wanted to become American citizens applied overseas. No one was coming through Ellis Island, so the government closed it. The buildings became run-down. Vandals smashed windows, the grass was overgrown, and rain fell through the holes in the roofs of the buildings.

But Ellis Island wasn't forgotten. It remained an important place in the history of both the United States and many American families. In 1965 it was declared part of the Statue of Liberty National Monument.

Starting in 1982, money was raised to repair the main building on Ellis Island and turn it into a museum. Eight years later, in September of 1990, Ellis Island opened its doors—as the Ellis Island Immigration Museum.

On an average day, thousands of people take ferries to Ellis Island. Visitors include tourists from around the world, school groups, families of immigrants, and many older people who were processed at Ellis Island. For these immigrants, the journey back to Ellis Island awakens many memories.

The museum's exhibits tell the story of immigration. With computers, photographs, and the immigrants' own words, the exhibits lead visitors along the path that the immigrants followed from one inspection to the next. Two

Visitors arrive in ferries to tour the Ellis Island Immigration Museum.

movie theaters show films about the immigration experience. Special phones are available for visitors to hear immigrants' tape-recorded stories.

In one exhibit, a play-worn teddy bear that a little girl brought across the ocean from Switzerland years ago stares out at visitors from its glass case. It is just one of the many treasured belongings that American families donated to the museum. Nearby, an old piano rests silently, its working parts ruined by moisture and time. It, too, is on display, along with several hundred items left behind when the building closed. These exhibits are a window into Ellis Island's past.

One of the most popular exhibits is just outside the museum, on the east side of the island. It's a long, low wall overlooking Manhattan. Etched into copper panels atop the wall are the names of immigrants—two hundred thousand in all. Behind each name is an inspiring story of bravery and courage. Together, the museum's exhibits tell the inspiring story of the peopling of America—the largest human migration in modern history.

CHAPTER 2

THE IMMIGRANTS' STORY

The Native American Indians are the earliest "immigrants" to have come to America. Thousands of years ago, they crossed a land bridge from Asia into America.

After many centuries, people from other lands began settling in the United States. They came in three "waves" of immigration. The first wave took place from 1600 to 1776. Most of these settlers were English, French, and Scottish, and they formed colonies up and down the Atlantic Coast. The second wave was from 1776 to 1890, and was mostly German, Dutch, and Irish people. The third wave took place from 1890 to 1924, and included many European Jews. This last wave was processed through Ellis Island.

These immigrants came by choice. But thousands of Africans were forced to come to this country. They traveled to America in chains, and at the end of their journey were sold as slaves. At that time, America did not promise a better life for them.

People uprooted themselves to come to America for many reasons. Some came to avoid starvation in their own countries. Ireland's massive immigration started in 1845, when Ireland's potato crop was infested with a disease called potato rot. Potatoes were the staple, or main food, of the Irish diet. Thousands of people starved. The people's only hope to survive was to leave their country. Almost two million Irish citizens emigrated to the United States during this time.

The Industrial Revolution, a time of great change throughout the world, caused many people to move. Factories were being built that could produce goods quickly and cheaply. The same cabinet that would take a carpenter days to construct took only hours by machine. Hand-craftsmen couldn't compete and many went out of business. During this time, almost sixty million people left their homes in Europe for other countries. Thirty-four million traveled to the United States. Here, growing industries needed workers and paid high wages.

In the 1880s, Eastern European Jews began coming to America in large numbers. They fled pogroms, or massacres, in their native lands as well as unfair laws.

All immigrants hoped that in their adopted country, their lives would be better. When she was four years old, Elizabeth Longfield came from a small farm in Yugoslavia with her mother. The family couldn't afford suitcases, so they loaded their belongings in a tablecloth and set off on the long journey.

Although most immigrants left hardships behind, it took a great deal of courage to say

In the late 1800s, a Norwegian woman bid farewell to her loved ones before leaving for America.

good-bye to their homes, loved ones, and friends. Most didn't speak English and knew little about American life. But, as Elizabeth's family had done, they bravely packed their belongings into bundles to seek a better life.

The ocean voyage took courage, too. Today, planes can cross the Atlantic in a few hours. Before 1870, though, wooden sailing ships took more than two months to make the same trip. Most of the immigrants could only afford the cheapest tickets, which cost about eight dollars—a lot at that time. They traveled in steerage, the bottom of the ship near its steering machinery.

Shipping companies that were eager to make money took on more passengers than they had room for. The immigrants slept in large, crowded rooms, in row after row of bunk beds. Only one hatch, or opening, let in sunlight and fresh air. During storms the hatch was closed for safety, and the passengers had to stay down below. It

A line drawing of immigrants who crossed the Atlantic in steerage, located at the bottom of the ship.

was frightening and many people became seasick. For the duration of the journey, even the air the passengers breathed was foul smelling.

Worse than the odor were the diseases. Cholera, dysentery, and typhus could spread rapidly among passengers. Death from disease was common on immigrant ships. In 1868, 105 of the 544 passengers died during the seventy-day voyage of the *Liebnitz,* a German ship. Inspectors who went on board the ship determined that the deaths had come about from several causes, including a lack of fresh air, cleanliness, medical care, water, and food.

The immigrants put up with the bad conditions, fearing that if they complained, they wouldn't be allowed to come to America. And most didn't speak the language of the ship's crew, either.

The coming of steamships in 1870 improved conditions for passengers. The steam-powered engines shortened travel time to about two weeks. By 1890 the trip was even quicker—just eight days. The United States government also had passed laws to protect immigrants' health. One law required steamships to provide more space in steerage to lower the risk of disease.

Seasickness was still hard to avoid, though. Elizabeth Longfield remembers that she and one other boy were the only two people in the dining

Immigrants crowded on deck to see their first glimpse of America.

room. The rest of the three hundred passengers were in their bunks, suffering from seasickness.

All managed to come up on deck, though, when America came into view. "We felt relief," recalled one woman from Poland. "It was like the doctor had given us a dose of happiness!"

Elizabeth and her fellow passengers had to be processed at Ellis Island by the federal gov-

Seeing the Statue of Liberty at last was a great relief after the long, difficult voyage.

ernment. Before 1892 immigrants entered at any seaport along the Atlantic Coast, and each state decided whether immigrants could settle in its borders. They had laws that kept out criminals, people with mental illnesses, and those who seemed unable to care for themselves. During the 1880s, though, the flood of immigrants to

America's ports became too much for the states to handle.

Government officials worried that over-worked state inspectors would let in people who would not be good for America. They did not want immigrants who would end up in jail or in a hospital. Also, dishonest boardinghouse own-ers, inspectors, and police officers were cheating many immigrants out of their money. The gov-ernment wanted the new Americans to be wel-comed, not robbed.

The federal government took charge of the immigration inspections in 1890. They decided to build a processing center on Ellis Island, since most immigrants entered America through New York City.

Ellis Island was a 3-acre (1.2-hectare) bar of mud and clay 1 mile (1.6 kilometers) south of Manhattan. The Native Americans had called it *Kilshk*, meaning Gull Island, after the sea gulls that nested there. Dutch people who settled in

New York during the seventeenth century called it Oyster Island, because they used it for harvesting oysters.

In the early eighteenth century, Ellis Island was called Gibbet Island. This was because pirates were hung there on gibbets, or gallows. During the American Revolution, a merchant and farmer, Samuel Ellis, owned the island and ran an inn on it.

In 1807 the government bought the island. They built a fort there and used it to defend the coast during the War of 1812 against the British. It was also used as a munitions depot—a place for storing ammunition and guns—for the navy.

By the time the government decided to turn Ellis Island into an immigration processing center, the fort had been abandoned for years. The workers' first task was to make the island bigger. They dropped boatloads of soil onto the 3-acre (1.2-hectare) island. Over the years, it would be increased in size to 27.5 acres (11.1

The original buildings of the immigration processing center on Ellis Island.

hectares). Workers dug a channel so that ferry-boats carrying immigrants could dock. They repaired some of the old fort's buildings and built new structures, including a hospital, mental institution, kitchen, dining hall, chapel, railway office, laundry, power plant, and dormitories (sleeping quarters).

In all, thirty-six buildings would be constructed. The most important one was a large wooden structure 400 feet (122 meters) long. This was the Registry Building, where each immigrant would be processed.

The building opened on January 1, 1892. Fifteen-year-old Annie Moore from Ireland was the first immigrant to pass through the Ellis Island Inspection Center. To celebrate the event, officials gave her a ten-dollar gold piece. Annie had never seen an American coin, the *New York Times* reported, and this was "the largest sum of money she had ever possessed."

About fifteen million immigrants followed Annie Moore through Ellis Island in the years that followed. Although they weren't given gold coins, each was eager to earn enough money to live freely and comfortably in the United States. And it was their hard work that helped build America.

CHAPTER 3

THE ISLAND OF HOPE— AND TEARS

Immigrants had to pass several inspections at Ellis Island. Many worried that if they answered an official's question incorrectly, they would be deported. The main building was also very crowded. To help the immigrants feel more comfortable, Americans from social organizations were on hand. They answered questions, gave toys to children and supported the bewildered immigrants through the inspection process.

The immigrants' luggage was inspected on the main floor. Then, guards shouting in many different languages separated the people into groups, and each was given a number. As the immigrants filed upstairs to the Registry Hall, doctors quickly looked them over. If someone

These newly arrived immigrants waited for inspections to begin.

seemed to have a health problem, doctors pulled
that person from the line. They marked the immigrant's clothing with a big chalk letter. *H*
stood for heart disease, *L* for lameness, *F* for
facial rash, and *X* for mental illness.

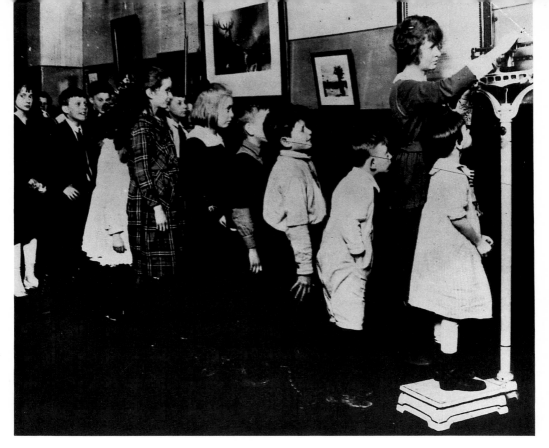

These children had their weight checked during inspections.

Another doctor lifted the immigrants' eyelids with a buttonhook, an old-fashioned tool for pulling buttons through buttonholes. In this frightening examination, the doctor looked for trachoma, an eye disease. People with medical problems would be deported, or sent back to their native lands. The doctors held back anyone wearing a chalk letter for closer examination.

One boy who had a facial rash because of an allergy to chocolate was held back. After five days, his rash cleared, so he was able to enter— on the promise not to eat chocolate any more.

The immigrants then moved through the two-story Registry Room. Beneath its high, curved ceiling, they waited in line to answer a long list of questions: What is your name? How much money do you have? Why did you come here? Do you have a job waiting for you? A law passed in 1882 made it illegal for anyone to be hired before coming to America.

Most immigrants completed their inspections in less than five hours. About one in six immigrants were held back, or detained. Some stayed for days or weeks, sleeping in crowded dormitories and eating in a large dining hall.

One Greek girl remembered the dormitories. "There was no place to get undressed to go to bed. Just lie down and sleep. And get up in the morning ready to travel."

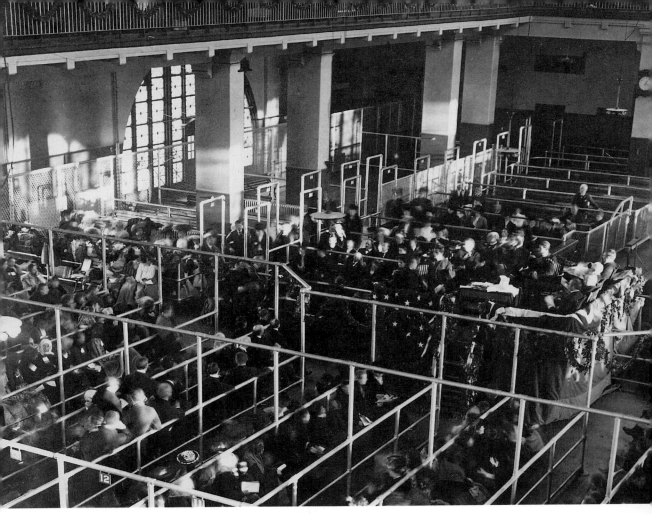

In the Registry Room, immigrants waited in line to answer a long list of questions.

In the dining hall, which seated one thousand people, immigrants tried foods that were new to them. Rievel Kaplan, who came from Lithuania, said, "I ate white bread and butter for the first time. I thought it was cake." Eliza-

Immigrants who were detained ate their meals in Ellis Island's large dining hall.

beth Longfield remembers eating her first orange. "I tried to eat it like an apple." Then, a woman told her to peel it.

Those who failed their inspections were often deported. It was very sad when one person from a family was declared not fit to enter the United States. The family then had to decide whether to stay together and go back home, or to separate.

In all, about 2 percent were deported. For these people, Ellis Island was the Island of Tears.

Ellis Island was the Island of Hope for the 98 percent of those who passed the inspections. These people received landing tickets, which stated their names and that they were allowed to enter the country. They traded in their foreign money for American dollars and bought railway tickets if they were headed west. Then they collected their luggage and took a ferry to the island of Manhattan. Some stayed there, while others left for cities and towns across America.

Many immigrants started their new lives in neighborhoods where friends or relatives from their homelands had settled. Whole sections of cities were often made up of people from a particular country. In Boston, New York, and other big cities, people could smell the cooking aromas coming from the houses and know what sort of neighborhood they were in. Some of these neighborhoods still bear names such as Little Italy or Chinatown, reminders of their immigrant past.

Many immigrants had been told that America's streets were paved with gold. One young Polish immigrant was advised to take a shovel— to shovel up the gold! The immigrants soon discovered that the streets weren't paved with gold. They found work in factories and mines, in the steel and automobile industries and on farms and railroads.

Although the immigrants worked long hours, most found that their lives were better in the United States. When they wrote home, whole villages gathered to hear word from the "promised land," as some called America.

"Here, you break your back for twelve hours a day," one Polish immigrant wrote. Even so, he wanted to stay. "Once you have tasted America, there is no way to go back to those old miseries." In the United States, this man's children could go to school for free. If he saved enough money, he could buy his own house, and send his children to college. In many European countries at that time, these things weren't possible.

Then, five years after Ellis Island opened, on June 15, 1897, fire broke out. It spread rapidly, and within three hours the main building and several others burned to the ground. Fortunately, few people were on the island and no one died. Within three years, the government had constructed a new and bigger immigration center. The buildings were of brick and concrete—so they would not burn.

In 1900, Theodore Roosevelt became president of the United States. He looked at the way immigrants were treated at Ellis Island and did not like what he saw. Many immigrants were being cheated. They were being shortchanged when they traded in their money, and the government hoped to end this practice. Many paid high prices at Ellis Island's dining hall for poor-quality food served on dirty plates. Roosevelt hired a new commissioner, William Williams, to run Ellis Island and told him to fire dishonest workers.

Williams "cleaned house" at Ellis Island, and hired more workers to process the increasing numbers of immigrants. Often, thousands of people passed through Ellis Island in a day. On one busy day in 1907, 11,747 people landed at the Island of Hope. The crowd resembled a fashion show from many different cultures. There were Slavic women dressed in colorful shawls, Dutch children in wooden shoes, and Orthodox Jewish men in black hats and coats. So many people had infants that one immigrant said, "The baby in the arms was almost like part of the costume."

President Roosevelt and William Williams tried to help the new immigrants feel at home. But there were many Americans who did not welcome foreigners. Workers who belonged to organizations called labor unions had struggled

This Italian immigrant family landed at the Island of Hope in 1900.

to secure better wages and working conditions. They feared that immigrants would work for less pay and take away their jobs. Some people said that immigrants, with their strange customs, would change the American way of life.

These fears led Congress to pass a "quota" law in 1921. This law limited the number of immigrants who could enter the United States each year from each country. The first year the law took effect, only 358,000 immigrants were allowed to come. This was a big drop from years past. In 1914 over twice that many had entered. And in 1907, the record year, 1.5 million people had emigrated. In 1929 Congress further dropped the total to 150,000.

World events also slowed the flow of immigration. During World War I, which started in 1914, the German navy sank the *Lusitania*, a passenger ship. Few people dared cross the ocean to America after that, fearing attacks.

From 1917 to 1918, while the United States

A Russian Jewish immigrant in his native dress of the early 1900s.

fought Germany in Europe, Ellis Island was used by the military. Captured crews of German ships were held there. The army also set up a wartime hospital of one thousand beds.

During this time, Americans began to fear

immigrants for a new reason. Communists—who believed that all citizens should share a nation's land and wealth equally—had toppled the Russian government in 1917. Many Americans argued that immigrants held harmful, "un-American" ideas, or were working against the United States government. Some foreign-born people who took part in political protests were arrested and detained on Ellis Island. In 1919 they began to be deported. By 1932, more people were deported from Ellis Island than entered the country there—twenty thousand were sent home, while only three thousand passed through.

The Great Depression of the 1930s, a time when jobs were scarce for all Americans, kept immigrants from coming to the United States. More people left the country than entered during this time. This changed just before World War II began. At that time, 250,000 people, including many Jews, fled from Adolf Hitler and his Nazi government in Germany.

America entered the war against Germany in 1941, and Ellis Island's buildings were again used by the military. When the war ended in 1945, millions of Europeans were left homeless. The United States passed the Displaced Persons Act, which allowed some of these refugees to settle in America.

The immigrants did not come through Ellis Island, though. All inspections were now completed overseas. The main building appeared empty and strangely quiet. The great immigration center was serving almost exclusively as a detention center.

On November 29, 1954, the government closed Ellis Island. The only ones who stayed behind were guards—to keep people from vandalizing the vacant buildings that had once bustled with activity.

CHAPTER 4

A New Life for Ellis Island

When the doors to Ellis Island's main building closed in 1954, the immigration center became a "ghost town." Furniture sat where it had been left, and papers lay scattered and untouched. A workman's cap rotted on the hook where it had been hung. No one disturbed the footprints that remained on the dusty floors.

Through the years, rain, wind, and snow caused roofs to collapse. In freezing weather, old water pipes burst open. Plaster fell from ceilings onto old hospital beds and washroom floors. Pieces of glass from broken windows sparkled in the rubble.

Ellis Island wasn't forgotten, though. Many immigrants had entered America through the

No one took care of the immigration center after it closed in 1954.

island. To these people and others, Ellis Island stood for the freedom and opportunities the United States offered to immigrants from around the world. President Lyndon B. Johnson agreed with them, and in 1965, he made Ellis Island part of the Statue of Liberty National Monument.

In 1976 the National Park Service began giving tours of the old, neglected main building on Ellis Island. That first year fifty thousand people visited. It was clear that people thought Ellis Island was an important historic place.

A growing number of public officials and private citizens wanted to restore Ellis Island's main building. Repairing the building, though, would cost a lot of money—money that the government didn't have.

In 1982 President Reagan formed the Statue of Liberty–Ellis Island Centennial Commission. This foundation would restore Ellis Island and the Statue of Liberty. To raise the money needed, they would turn to the American people. President Reagan named Lee Iacocca, chairman of the Chrysler Corporation, as its head.

Iacocca's parents had passed through Ellis Island from Italy to the United States years before. He gladly took charge of the fund-raising effort. He called it a "labor of love for my mother and father."

Businesses, organizations, and citizens pitched in. The Advertising Council, Inc. of New York, Washington, D.C., and Los Angeles gave the foundation a free advertising campaign. The Disabled Veterans contributed one million dollars to provide ramps and elevators for people in wheelchairs.

The same organizations that had offered advice and social services to immigrants on Ellis Island years ago helped out again. They called their friends and asked them to give money. Polish Americans, Greek Americans, Italian Americans, and other ethnic groups held raffles,

dinners, and dances to raise funds. Schools, Boy
Scouts, and Girl Scouts took part in bake sales
and walkathons.

The foundation raised 136 million dollars,
but even that wasn't enough. Then Lee Iacocca
came up with a brilliant way to raise money—
and honor immigrants at the same time. The
idea was to create the American Immigrant Wall
of Honor. For every one hundred dollars a person donated, he or she could have an immigrant
family member's name engraved on a wall sur-
rounding the island. Twenty million dollars in
donations flooded into the foundation, enough
for two hundred thousand immigrant names—
and enough to begin work on the museum. In
1984 the largest restoration project in American
history began.

The museum's planners wanted the main
building to appear as it did in the early twentieth century. Architects studied eighty-year-old
photographs to learn how the building looked at

Restoration began in 1984.

that time. Computers analyzed the paint chips from the walls so that painters could match the building's original color.

Engineers studied the building's original construction materials, so they could match them as closely as possible. They had to figure out how to make some materials all over again. The recipe for a plaster called Caen Stone that was used in the Registry Room had been lost. Engineers experimented until they came up with the right formula. Half of the copper trim on the roofs had fallen down and rusted. It had to be copied exactly and replaced. Soot had to be cleaned off the building's exterior.

Historians investigated the main building room by room, salvaging everything they could, including old furniture, objects left behind by immigrants, official immigration papers, and washroom sinks. Most of these artifacts would become part of the museum's exhibits. The old sinks would be installed in the museum's new bathrooms.

The restoration team gathered old photographs and documents to include in the museum's exhibits. Families donated objects that their ancestors had taken with them from their native countries.

The museum's planners also added special features to the restored site. They installed com-

Historians salvaged everything they could find that remained at Ellis Island, including old silverware.

puters which would tell the story of immigration through different games. With money donated from the William Randolph Hearst Foundation, the planners created an oral history studio for people to listen to recordings of immigrants' stories. They established a library full of books on immigration, old records that clerks had kept on immigrants' inspections, and other docu-

Men and women wearing ethnic costumes paraded by the Ellis Island Immigration Museum on its opening day in September 1990.

ments. A sixteen-screen VideoWall donated by the NYNEX Corporation would become a learning center for school groups.

The opening date for the Ellis Island Immigration Museum was set for September 10, 1990. So many people wanted to attend the dedication ceremony that there wasn't enough room for them all. The foundation held a drawing, and those whose names were picked were allowed to attend. Hundreds of people watched a parade of men and women in the costumes of foreign countries. They listened to the music by the United States Army Band.

Former immigrants, government officials, the museum's planners, and business leaders took part in the ceremony. Ellis Island had been restored to its rightful place—as one of the most important monuments to the American heritage.

CHAPTER 5

ELLIS ISLAND TODAY

On a sunny April morning in 1991, the Ellis Island ferry docked at Battery Park at the south end of Manhattan Island. A crowd of over one thousand people surged forward, anxious to get on board. Guards kept order and counted each person who stepped onto the ferry. One helped the elderly people who had trouble walking up the ship's ramp. In all, nine hundred people boarded, and then the guard closed the railing. The three-tiered ship was full.

The ferry sailed away from Manhattan. It circled the Statue of Liberty but did not stop. It was headed for Ellis Island. The people on board were not immigrants, though. They were coming to visit the Ellis Island Immigration Museum.

Tourists from England, Japan, Italy, and other countries, families, and schoolchildren crowded around the railings. An elderly man gazed out at the island, with tears in his eyes. He had come through Ellis Island from Germany when he was six years old, and was remembering the first time he set foot in America.

The trip to Ellis Island is inspiring to all visitors, whether they are visiting the island for the first time or reliving their own immigrant experience. As the ferry pulls into Ellis Island Harbor, visitors see an old wooden ferry sunken in the water. This boat was used to take immigrants to Ellis Island eighty years ago.

From the ferry, visitors walk up the sidewalk toward a large brick building, the Ellis Island Immigration Museum. With its high, arched windows, four spires, and shining copper trim, it resembles a palace. Years earlier, people from 170 nations entered that same building, each hoping to start a new life.

A ferry filled with tourists pulls into Ellis Island Harbor.

From the moment visitors pass through the main building's doors, they start to feel what it was like to be an immigrant coming to America. In the center of the room is a display filled with immigrants' luggage. Officials inspected millions of bags here. Wooden trunks that look like treasure chests and huge wicker baskets are piled on top of each other. Each was once filled with the belongings that the immigrants chose to take with them from their countries.

Beyond this display is the "Peopling of America" exhibit, located in the old railroad office. Here, immigrants purchased special train tickets to destinations across America. Now, computers and colorful displays tell the story of immigration from the 1600s to the present day. The routes that people followed light up on a globe that is 6 feet (1.82 meters) across.

A huge computerized map of the United States shows where immigrants of 122 different nationalities settled. Visitors enter a nationality, such as Italian, and the number of Italian Americans living in each of the fifty states is highlighted on the electronic map. When visitors push one button, they can see how Irish and Italians moved along the Erie Canal into New York state. Another button shows them that Scandinavians traveled to the copper mines and timber companies of the upper Midwest.

From this exhibit, visitors can go to the Registry Room on the second floor. Although this room is the largest in the building, it is almost empty. During the busy years of immigration, it bustled with people. Shouts and questions in many languages echoed from its walls. Today, a few wooden benches where immigrants waited remain on the red tile floor.

American flags hang from the balcony, where doctors used to spot-check immigrants. The Registry Room is a memorial to all immigrants who came to the United States, whether they entered through Ellis Island or elsewhere.

The museum's designers wanted the Registry Room to be a place for quiet thought. Here, they hoped visitors would be able to imagine immigrants' hopes and fears. Some people feel strong emotions in the Registry Room. They feel very close to the immigrants, almost as if the room were haunted by ghosts.

In the West Wing next to the Great Hall is

the fourteen-room exhibit titled "Through America's Gate." Here, people went through further inspections. Doctors looked closely at people with chalk letters on their clothing. In another area are the tests—in twelve different languages—immigrants took to see if they could read. After 1917, if immigrants could not read, a law required that they be deported.

The Board of Inquiry room appears as it did in the early twentieth century. Immigrants who had been detained had to explain to the board why they shouldn't be sent back to their homelands.

While most of the museum's walls have been painted a clean, buttery yellow, the old surface was left untouched in this area. Visitors see the graffiti that immigrants left on the walls. One immigrant waiting to appear before the board scribbled these words in Greek: Cursed be the day I left my homeland. Another, possibly a farmer, sketched a chicken and a cow.

A door in the corner of the Registry Room leads to a dormitory. In that small room, forty people slept crowded together on row after row of narrow cots. There were many such dormitories on Ellis Island.

In the second floor's East Wing is the ten-room exhibit, "Peak Immigration Years, 1880-1924." These displays follow the immigrants' journey from distant European villages and seaports to the United States.

Passports, steamship tickets, and lists of ships' passengers line the walls. Old advertisements for everything from entertainment to English classes hang from the ceiling. Historic photographs help tell the story, too. Visitors look into the faces of an immigrant girl working in an American textile mill and Chinese workers picking fruit in California.

Computers that give a citizenship test for immigrants are available for visitors, too. There's a telephone that doesn't dial out, but

Old graffiti on a pillar in the main building, drawn and written years ago by immigrants.

Many American families donated their ancestors' heirlooms to the museum to be included in exhibits.

rather tunes in to different immigrants' stories, which have been recorded in the Oral History Studio.

The exhibit on the third floor, called "Treasures from Home," displays over one thousand objects and photographs that the immigrants brought with them. Often, immigrants could take only what they could carry to America, so they packed their most cherished possessions. Some of these became heirlooms, lovingly passed on from one generation to the next. Many American families donated their heirlooms to the museum.

Among the objects on display are a child's intricately embroidered dress from Poland, a stringed musical instrument called a *zither* from Norway, and a sewing machine from England. There is a donkey's shoe that was given to an Irish immigrant by his father as a good luck charm, and a piece of coral an immigrant brought with her from Cyprus. It served as a reminder of a seaside home left far behind.

The William Randolph Hearst Oral History Studio, on the third floor, is where visitors can listen to American immigrants' recorded stories of what it was like to cross the ocean, pass through Ellis Island, and settle in the United States. Oral historians walk through the museum, answering questions and handing out questionnaires. The forms are for the Oral History Project, in which all living immigrants who were processed at Ellis Island can participate. The head historian, Paul Seacrest, interviews some of these immigrants and records their stories.

Most visitors view the film the museum offers on Ellis Island. The Learning Center is another popular stop. Here, school groups watch a sixteen-screen VideoWall and play games to learn about the immigrant experience.

The most popular exhibit isn't inside the building, though. It's the American Immigrant Wall of Honor, which stretches along the east side of the island. Etched into its 465 panels are names of 200,000 immigrants. Each person remembered on this wall—from Mary Sullivan of Ireland to Domenico Preziosi of Italy—emigrated to the United States. The wall honors all immigrants who uprooted themselves to seek freedom and opportunity here.

The American Immigrant Wall of Honor.

Today, immigrants are still coming to America for the same reasons. Many had no chance to achieve their goals in their native lands. The United States now permits 270,000 immigrants to enter the country each year. The immigration process begins overseas, where people apply to come to the United States. Instead of the hours or days it took at Ellis Island, the entire process can take months or years.

When today's immigrants talk about life in the United States, they sound like the people who landed at Ellis Island years ago. "I work hard, and it is good to work hard when there is reason to do so," said a young man from Cuba. "It was hard, very hard to walk away from the friends of a lifetime and all of the things we owned," recalled a Czech woman. "We always wanted to live in a democracy," she continued, "and that is why we thought of America."

Ellis Island:
A Historical Time Line

1890   The United States government selects Ellis
Island as the site of its new immigration
center in New York City.

1892   The immigration center on Ellis Island begins
processing new immigrants.

1897   Fire destroys the buildings on Ellis Island;
everyone on the island escapes harm.

1900   A new brick immigration center opens on Ellis
Island.

1917-
1919   During World War I, Ellis Island serves as an
army hospital and a holding place for captured
German seamen.

1919   Ellis Island becomes a deportation center as
well as an immigration center.

1954   The immigration center on Ellis Island closes.

1965   President Lyndon B. Johnson signs a formal
statement adding Ellis Island to the Statue of
Liberty National Monument.

1976   Ellis Island opens for visitors.

1982   President Ronald Reagan asks Lee Iacocca to
lead a drive to restore Ellis Island and the
Statue of Liberty.

1984   Ellis Island closes to visitors; the restoration
work begins.

1990   The restored main building opens again as the
Ellis Island Immigration Museum.

WELL-KNOWN PEOPLE WHO ENTERED THE UNITED STATES AT ELLIS ISLAND

Issac Asimov (1920-   ) *Homeland, Russia.* Author of many books of science and science fiction.

Irving Berlin (1888-1989) *Homeland, Russia.* Composer of many popular songs, including "White Christmas," "God Bless America," and "The Easter Parade."

Samuel Chotzinoff (1889-1964) *Homeland, Russia.* Pianist, music critic, and radio personality.

Father Edward Flanagan (1886-1948) *Homeland, Ireland.* A Roman Catholic priest who founded Boys Town, Nebraska, a residence for homeless boys.

Felix Frankfurter (1882-1965) *Homeland, Austria.* U.S. Supreme Court justice; professor of law at Harvard University in Cambridge, Massachusetts.

Samuel Goldwyn (1882-1974) *Homeland, Poland.* Movie producer; one of the founders of MGM Studios.

Bob Hope (1903-   ) *Homeland, England.* Actor and comedian.

Al Jolson (1886-1950) *Homeland, Russia.* Singer and actor; starred in *The Jazz Singer*, the first motion picture with sound.

Charles "Lucky" Luciano (1897-1962) *Homeland, Italy.* Well-known criminal of the 1920s; later deported from Ellis Island.

Bela Lugosi (1882-1956) *Homeland, Hungary.*
Movie actor famed for portraying Count Dracula.

Golda Meir (1898-1978) *Homeland, Russia.* Prime
Minister of Israel.

Solomon Rabinowitz (1859-1916) *Homeland,
Russia.* Short-story writer and playwright; wrote
many stories about country life in Russia under the
pen name Shalom Aleichem; the musical play *Fiddler on the Roof* was based on some of his stories.

Hyman Rickover (1900-1986) *Homeland, Russia.*
U.S. Navy admiral; helped to develop nuclear-powered submarines.

Edward G. Robinson (1893-1973) *Homeland,
Romania.* Movie actor best known for portraying a
tough-talking criminal.

Knute Rockne (1888-1931) *Homeland, Norway.*
Football coach at Notre Dame University in Indiana.

Baron Georg von Trapp (1879-1947), **Maria von
Trapp** (1905-1987), **and family** *Homeland,
Austria.* The singing von Trapp family portrayed in
The Sound of Music.

Visitor Information

Transportation

Ferry service to Ellis Island is available at Battery Park in lower Manhattan. From April through November, ferries also run between Ellis Island and Liberty State Park in Jersey City, New Jersey.

Hours

Open every day except Christmas; the first ferries leave Battery Park and Liberty State Park at 9:00 A.M. The last ferries leave Ellis Island at approximately 5:30 P.M. Due to crowds, the wait at the dock may be long in warm weather.

Admission

There is no admission charge to enter Ellis Island. However, the ferryboat fee is $3 for children ages 3 through 11 and $6 for older children and adults. No fare is charged for children under the age of 3. Free shuttle service is provided between Ellis Island and Liberty Island, site of the Statue of Liberty.

Additional information can be obtained from:

Ellis Island National Park Service
New York, NY 10004
(212) 363-3200 (general information)
(212) 269-5755 (ferry schedules and fare information)
(212) 363-8833; (212) 363-8834 (information on using the William Randolph Hearst Oral History Studio or Library for Immigration Studies)

Index